Mr. Yowder and the Windwagon

Other "Mr. Yowder" Books by Glen Rounds

Mr. Yowder
and the
Windwagon

written and illustrated by

GLEN ROUNDS

Holiday House / New York

Library of Congress Cataloging in Publication Data

Rounds, Glen, 1906–
Mr. Yowder and the windwagon.

Summary: Mr. Yowder tries to make his fortune by
inventing a real prairie schooner from sails, a mast,
a rudder, and an old wagon, but makes a mess instead.
{1. Tall tales.   2. West (U.S.)—Fiction.   3. Wagons—
Fiction}   I. Title.
PZ7.R761Mm   1983   {Fic}   83-6183
ISBN 0-8234-0499-4

To Anna, my little sister,
with much love, even after all these years

It all happened many, many years ago. But, as he himself told the story later, Mr. Xenon Zebulon Yowder's famous adventure with the Windwagon came about because of a job of work he did for a Missouri River steamboat captain.

It seems that Mr. Yowder was wintering in St. Louis, which in those days was known as the Gateway to the West, and one afternoon towards spring he happened into conversation with a man painting one of the many steamboats tied to the riverbank at the edge of town.

The man introduced himself as Captain Pernell P. Proudfoot, which was also the name of the boat he was painting.

"Every steamboat has to have a name," the captain explained, "and when I bought this one I decided to name it for myself because people feel safer riding with a captain who also owns his own steamboat."

When Mr. Yowder remarked that it was a mighty handsome boat, what with the new coat of white paint and all, but that it would look even better with its name painted on it, the captain told him that he was already looking for a good sign painter to do just that.

So Mr. Yowder explained that he himself was known far and wide as "The World's Bestest and Fastest Sign Painter," and that he'd be right pleased to figure on the job.

So after they'd agreed on a price Mr. Yowder went back to the boardinghouse for his paint box and started work that very day.

On the front of the pilothouse he painted THE PERNELL P. PROUDFOOT in gold letters almost a foot high. Then he added outlines, shading and all manner of fancy curlicues in blue, green, yellow and red.

And on the great paddle wheel covers on either side of the steamboat he painted the name again in even bigger and fancier letters. Altogether it took him the best part of a week, but when he'd finished, the Proudfoot was easily the flashiest looking steamboat on the whole Missouri River. And Captain Proudfoot was so pleased with the job that he not only paid Mr. Yowder a couple dollars extra but invited him to ride along on his next trip up the river to Westport Landing—three hundred miles farther west.

"Westport is booming these days," he explained. "Full of people fitting out their prairie schooners for the trip across the Plains to Santa Fe, Oregon or the California gold fields. And there isn't a sign painter in all that part of the country."

Now Mr. Yowder had been sort of planning on spending the summer painting signs and seeing old friends down in Arkansas, or maybe Tennessee. But at that time he'd never seen the Great Plains and, besides, he was curious about the prairie schooners the captain spoke of. So it turned out that when the Pernell P. Proudfoot pulled out of St. Louis a week later, Mr. Yowder was on board.

As the steamboat chuffed its way slowly up the muddy, crooked river he and Captain Proudfoot played endless games of checkers, drank lemonade or simply leaned on the rail watching the scenery.

When they finally tied up at Westport, Mr. Yowder found the place was as busy as the captain had said it was. Everywhere he looked outside the town, he saw camps of people getting ready to cross the Plains.

And in the town itself there were men selling and repairing wagons. Others sold or traded mules, oxen and horses while still others provided maps, ropes, beans, and coffee and supplies of a hundred kinds. And all of them wanted signs painted, so Mr. Yowder soon had all the work he could do.

But he was disappointed to find that the so-called prairie schooners were only big, creaking, canvas-covered wagons drawn by slow-moving strings of horses or oxen.

Then one afternoon when he'd quit work early and ridden out to the edge of the Plains to shoot a couple of grouse for his supper, he came onto the top of a little rise beside the Santa Fe Trail just as a long line of freight wagons was disappearing over the horizon. And as he watched them rocking slowly along, with the

wind whipping and billowing their white canvas covers, he suddenly realized that they *did* look like a line of sailing ships on a rolling brown ocean!

When they were finally out of sight he rode slowly back to his camp, thinking furiously. And all the time he was cooking and eating his supper he continued to think. He knew that Santa Fe was nearly a thousand miles away, and it would take those wagons months to make the trip. He'd noticed that the wind blew constantly across the Plains, as it did over the ocean, so why wouldn't it be possible to put masts and sails on the big wagons and make them into *real* prairie schooners? By using wind power to replace the slow oxen, the trips could be made in weeks—or even days.

Of course he realized that the rolling plains were not quite as smooth as they looked. However, the time he'd rented a rowboat and gone fishing in New York City years ago, he'd discovered that the ocean itself was mighty rough when you got out towards the middle. And in spite of that, as everybody knows, ships had been sailing back and forth across it for years and years.

So Mr. Yowder decided to go into business and already was dreaming of whole fleets of wind-powered wagons racing across the Plains like small clipper ships carrying freight and passengers from place to place. At first he considered calling his sailing wagons "Real Prairie Schooners" but, after some thought, decided "Windwagon" was a catchier name.

But next day when he spoke to some Possible Investors about the great profits to be made in the freight-hauling business by replacing the slow, expensive oxteams with sails and wind power, they said it would never work.

They agreed that ox-drawn wagons were slow, and that it did take months to get a load of freight to or from Santa Fe. But, they asked, if moving wagons by wind power was possible why hadn't it been done before? And one by one they put their hands in their pockets and walked away.

Even though no one took his idea seriously Mr. Yowder was still convinced that swiftly moving Windwagons would one day replace oxteams on the Plains as the steamboats had replaced the clumsy keelboats on the rivers not so long ago. He remembered the trouble Fulton had had trying to convince people that the steamboat was practical.

So he decided to give up sign painting for a while and build the first Windwagon himself. However, he didn't have a wagon to start with and even the second-hand ones on Honest Henry's lot cost more than he could afford. But some time before, he'd taken an odd buggy in trade for a sign, so he decided to start out with a Windbuggy, then go on to a full-sized Windwagon later.

He found a long pole and set it up behind the seat for a mast, nailing it firmly in place and bracing it with scraps of old boards and rope he found lying about. From other scraps he made a sort of rudder to steer with, and for a sail he cut up an old wagon cover some emigrant had thrown away.

All this naturally attracted considerable attention, especially when he'd painted YOWDER'S PATENTED WINDBUGGY in big red and yellow letters on the rudder. Of course the thing wasn't really patented, but Mr. Yowder thought it would sort of look official.

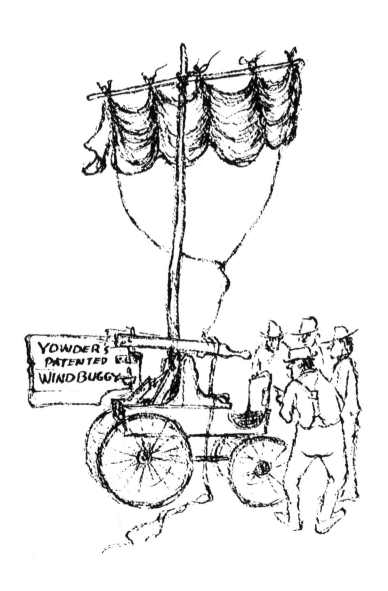

The people still didn't take his idea seriously. But nonetheless a good-sized crowd was on hand the morning Mr. Yowder took the finished Windbuggy out for its trial run. Climbing into the seat he took a firm grip on the rudder handle, raised the sail and waved to the crowd as the canvas caught the wind and the strange-looking contraption began to move.

With the wind behind him Mr. Yowder and the Windbuggy were soon traveling at a brisk pace, and gaining speed every minute. Holding his hat on with one hand and the rudder handle with the other Mr. Yowder figured this was as close as anyone could come to flying. And surely, now that the people had seen what wind power could do, they would begin to take his idea seriously.

He was just thinking of circling back to his starting place when he saw, straight ahead, the parked wagons of an emigrant camp. Women, busy tending fires under washpots and stringing clotheslines between the wagons, began to scream as Mr. Yowder pushed on the rudder handle to turn the buggy away. But he found that the makeshift rudder didn't work quite as well as he'd expected and the Windbuggy had no brakes, so without slowing down he drove straight into the middle of a line of flapping wash and on between the wagons, with the whole wash line flying behind him like the tail of a kite.

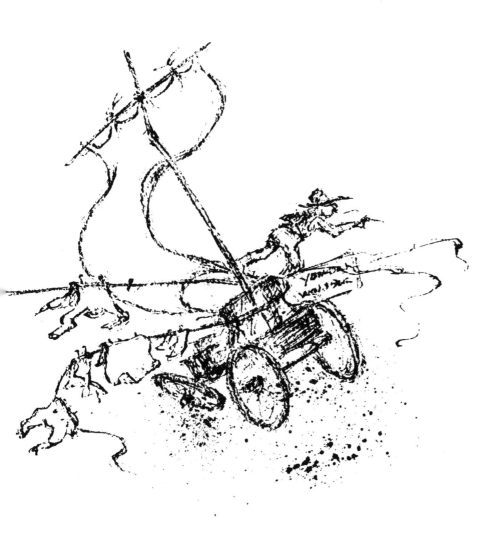

As he came out from between the wagons the rudder finally began to take hold and for a moment it looked as if Mr. Yowder had the Windbuggy under control at last. But as soon as he'd turned broadside to the wind, the weight of the top-heavy sail and tall mast upset the light buggy and it went over with a crash.

Mr. Yowder wasn't hurt, but his Windbuggy was a total wreck.

When he'd untangled himself from the wreckage Mr. Yowder apologized politely to the women for messing up their wash, but explained to the men that he guessed he'd showed them what wind power could do. He admitted that he should have realized that a mast and sail would make the light buggy too top-heavy—but that that would be no problem with full-sized wagons, for it is almost impossible to tip one of them over. So now, he told them, all he needed was for a few Investors to finance the cost of building a full-sized Windwagon, and he'd be in business.

But the Possible Investors still didn't take his idea seriously. They laughed, took another look at the wreck of the Windbuggy, then put their hands in their pockets and slowly walked away.

Even though his first experiment had not been a real success, Mr. Yowder still believed that Windwagons would soon be as common on the Plains as camels are on the Sahara. So instead of giving the idea up he set out to build a full-sized Windwagon himself.

Mr. Yowder still didn't have money enough to buy a wagon to start with, but out on the edge of the Plains were all manner of things discarded by the emigrants. There were pots and pans, furniture, parts of harness, ox yokes, scraps of clothing and even broken-down wagons. So by taking a good wheel from one and something else from another, Mr. Yowder had soon put together a wagon almost as good as new, and it hadn't cost him a cent.

At the back of the wagon, above the canvas cover, he built a high platform he called the Poop Deck and figured he'd drive the Windwagon from there. Instead of steering with a rudder this time, he decided to use a long pole like the steering sweep on the old flat boats. And for sudden stops he salvaged an old anchor from a wrecked steamboat down on the riverbank, and hung it from a bracket up at the front end.

So far he'd built everything from old scraps he'd found here and there. But for the sail he drew some money out of his savings and bought new canvas from a store in town.

Every now and again Mr. Yowder had had to stop work on the Windwagon and paint a few signs to make money to buy groceries or a few cans of paint, so the job took longer than he'd figured.

But finally the great day came when the Wind-wagon was finished and ready for its first demonstration run, and it was really a sight to see. The canvas of the wagon cover and the furled sail were white as snow, the wagon box was painted blue with white trim, and the wheels were fire-engine red with fine yellow striping. Even the anchor, swinging from its bracket, was painted red, white and blue. And as a finishing touch Mr. Yowder had painted *YOWDER'S WINDWAGON* in fancy letters on each side of the wagon box.

Along with a few other Possible Investors, Mr. Yowder had invited the Mayor of Westport, the Presidents of both of the town's banks and a visiting Senator from Illinois to ride on this first Windwagon trip.

When these Important People finally drove up he shook hands with them, helped them up the gangplank and seated them in chairs he'd borrowed and set up inside the wagon. He even rolled the bottom edges of the canvas cover up a few inches on either side so the passengers could watch the scenery as they rode.

After they were all seated he hauled in the gang-plank, climbed to the Poop Deck, set the big sail and took a firm grip on the end of the long steering sweep. For a moment the sail strained and popped in the wind and the tall mast creaked and groaned—but nothing else happened. Then, slowly at first, the Windwagon began to move!

Gaining speed it quickly left the cheering crowd behind, while the Mayor, the Bank Presidents and the other Possible Investors clapped each other on the back or waved to the riders galloping along side. And by the time it disappeared over the first low swell of prairie, trailing long clouds of dust, even the horsemen had been left behind.

The Santa Fe Trail had never before seen such speed. The rocking and jouncing of the Windwagon as it raced along the rough road made it difficult for the passengers to keep their chairs upright, and the Bank Presidents had trouble with the wind blowing their tall silk hats off. But they were all so excited by the unbelievable speed that they didn't seem to mind.

Standing braced on the high Poop Deck, holding onto his hat with one hand and the end of the steering sweep with the other, Mr. Yowder had just started singing an old sea chantey when he saw a long line of freight wagons moving along the trail ahead. He quickly overtook them and without slowing down, he leaned on the steering sweep to swing the Windwagon off the road. And as he passed close alongside, his passengers waved their hats and shouted to the startled freighters.

The sight of a wagon passing them with such speed—and without horses or oxen—was considerable of a shock to the men as well as the their usually placid teams. And when Mr. Yowder looked back from the top of the next ridge, he saw behind him a confused mass of plunging, bellowing oxen, tangled in their chains among overturned wagons, spilled freight, and frantically shouting men.

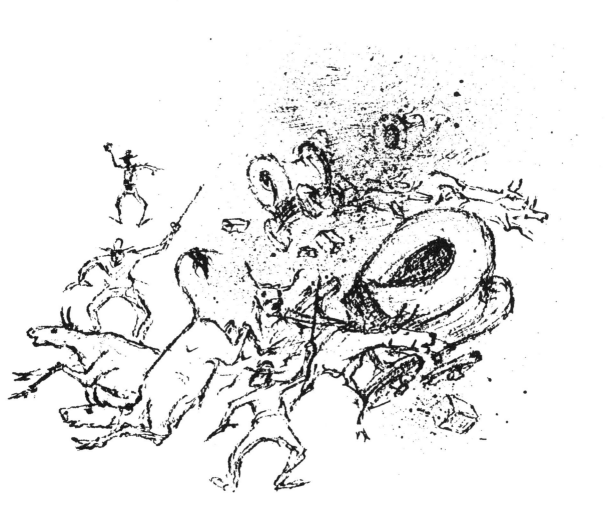

When Mr. Yowder started out that morning he intended to take the Possible Investors only a short way down the Santa Fe Trail before circling back to town. But now he was so pleased with the way the Windwagon was sailing—even better than he'd expected—that he decided to go a few miles farther, to give his passengers a ride they'd never forget.

Down the slope ahead was the wide, shallow river crossing, and he steered straight for it. Throwing great sheets of water as high as the Poop Deck, the Windwagon lurched and swayed across the rocky ford and up the farther bank without slowing in the least.

But halfway across the river the passengers had begun a great clamor from inside the wagon. As near as Mr. Yowder could make out, they wanted him to stop and let them off. However, he was having his own troubles at the time trying to steer the Windwagon along the narrow deep-washed ruts of the old road, so he paid them no mind. Anyway, he intended to stop as soon as he came to level ground again and let them all get out and walk around a bit before he took them back to town.

But when he got to the ridge and looked ahead he saw that the entire plain was covered with buffalo— thousands and thousands of them. His first thought was to stop the Windwagon by dropping the sail, but he found that the knots in the sail ropes had pulled so tight he couldn't undo them. So in desperation he dropped the anchor instead. But anchors are made to take hold in muddy sea or river bottoms and do not work satisfactorily on hard, dry prairie. So, with the useless anchor bouncing and bounding behind at the end of its rusty chain, the Windwagon continued to rush straight for the startled herd.

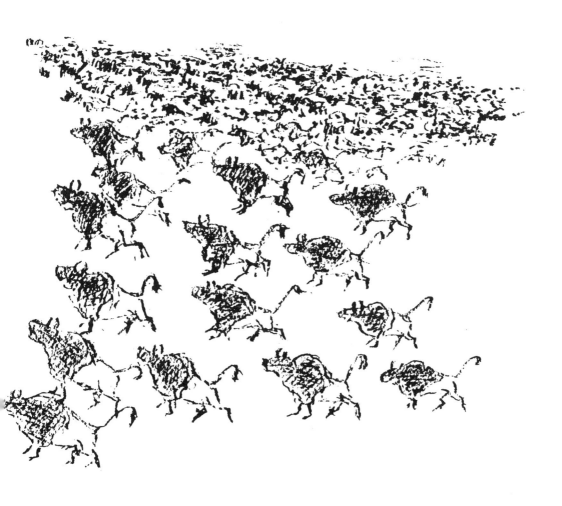

For a moment the buffalo stood frozen in their tracks as the Windwagon, with its sail flapping and axles screeching, came down the slope towards them. Then every animal in the herd wheeled and ran.

But in almost no time at all the speeding Windwagon had overtaken the stragglers and was plowing its
way into the thick of the great herd. Everywhere Mr.
Yowder looked he saw buffalo running with their heads
down and their tails curled over their backs. There were
buffalo behind him, on both sides of him and as far as
he could see ahead. So all he could do was steer the
Windwagon straight ahead and hope for the best.

Down the slope the Windwagon and the great herd went, and on down a wide valley, between two rows of low hills. The Possible Investors had suddenly stopped their complaining and were simply hanging onto the edges of the wagon box as best they could, hoping the thing wouldn't overturn.

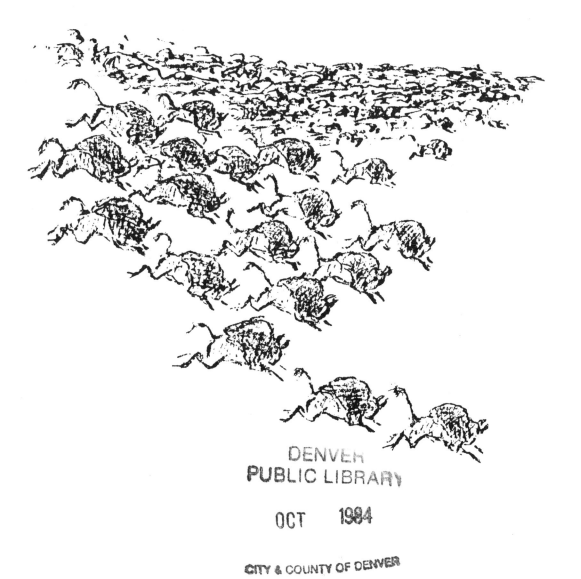

Being faster than the stampeding buffalo the
Windwagon was steadily moving up towards the front
of the stampeding herd, and Mr. Yowder hoped that
when he'd outrun the leaders they'd all turn and go
back the way they'd come. He thought of trying again
to untie the jammed sail rope knots, but was afraid that
if he stopped the wagon the buffalo coming from behind would upset it. Anyway, he was kept pretty busy
making sure the steering sweep didn't get tangled in the
dragging anchor chain.

Looking ahead Mr. Yowder saw an Indian war party ride into the valley in front of the leaders of the herd. Seeing the stampeding buffalo bearing down on them, the Indians whipped their horses to even greater speed and escaped just as the main herd, with the Windwagon sailing in its middle, thundered between them and the soldiers who had just come in sight on the farther ridge.

As the Windwagon and the buffalo passed in front
of the soldiers on the hill Mr. Yowder waved to them,
but they didn't wave back. Even after the last buffalo
was out of sight, and the dust had begun to settle, they
still sat their horses, wondering if they'd really seen
what they'd seen.

They knew that the General would be unhappy
about their letting the Indians escape, and they were
afraid he'd not believe their story when they told him
that they'd seen a wagon sailing like a ship in the middle of a great herd of stampeding buffalo. But they finally agreed they'd seen what they'd seen, and the Indians were long gone, so they turned their horses and
rode slowly towards the fort where they lived.

Meanwhile, far down the valley, Mr. Yowder had finally steered the Windwagon past the herd's leaders. And as he'd hoped, once they saw the Windwagon ahead of them the buffalo all turned and ran another way.

Out on the open plain again, with the Windwagon still sailing at full speed, Mr. Yowder let it steer itself while he worked to loosen the jammed knots in the sail ropes.

His passengers were making a fuss again, hollering for him to stop and let them off. Mr. Yowder called down to them that he was going to stop in just a minute—just as soon as he got the knots untied.

He had untied one and was just loosening the other, ready to drop the sail and bring the Windwagon to a stop, when the front wheels dropped into one of the deep washouts common in that country. The mast broke loose, carrying away the sail, while the Windwagon turned end over end and landed on its back.

Luckily nobody was hurt, except for some bruises and torn clothes—and a badly crushed silk hat belonging to one of the Bank Presidents. But the Windwagon was so badly torn up that Mr. Yowder knew it would never sail again.

When his passengers had dusted themselves off and poked the worst of the dents out of their hats they arranged themselves into a committee to ask Mr. Yowder how he figured to get them out of what they called "This Wilderness." And when he told them not to worry, he was about to signal for help, and they asked how in the world he could signal anybody from the middle of the Great Plains, he didn't bother to answer them.

Walking sadly over to the wreckage of the Windwagon, he gathered an armful of splinters and dried grass for kindling and set it afire. Soon what was left of the brightly painted wagon box, the canvas cover and the sail were blazing, sending a big column of black smoke high into the sky.

The soldiers, still only a few miles away, saw it and turned aside to investigate. When they rode up and found Mr. Yowder and his passengers gathered around the blazing wreckage of the Windwagon, they offered to take them up behind them on their horses for the trip back to the fort.

When they arrived at the fort, the General was very pleased to see them, for he didn't often have visitors, and invited them to have supper with him and stay overnight.

By the time they'd finished eating, the Possible Investors were in a much better humor. Leaning back in their chairs with glasses of lemonade in their hands they soon had the General in stitches as they told him about Mr. Yowder's harebrained Windwagon scheme and told of the things that had happened on their ride that day.

Mr. Yowder still insisted that Windwagons were the coming thing—but admitted that for now he was going to give the idea up and go back to sign painting.

The next morning after breakfast the General had one of his soldiers hitch up a team and haul the Possible Investors back to town in a spring wagon. As he shook hands with them he said it had been the finest visit he'd had in a long time—what with the story of the Windwagon and all—and invited them to come out to see him anytime.

Mr. Yowder, however, didn't leave with the others. Instead, he spent several weeks around the fort, painting signs for the General. And where he went after that, no one seems to know for sure.

And that is the TRUE STORY of how the Windwagon tale really started.